THERE'S A GOBLIN ON THE ARK!

by **Susan Tarcov**

illustrated by **Mackinzie Rekers**

APPLES & HONEY PRESS

For Marianne, who loved to tell the story of the good man named Noah.
—S.T.

To my favorites: Oliver, Emelia, and Finn.
—M.R.

Apples & Honey Press
An Imprint of Behrman House Publishers
Millburn, New Jersey 07041

www.applesandhoneypress.com

ISBN 978-1-68115-602-6

Library of Congress Cataloging-in-Publication Data
Names: Tarcov, Susan, author. | Rekers, Mackinzie, illustrator.
Title: There's a goblin on the ark! / by Susan Tarcov ; illustrated by
   Mackinzie Rekers.
Description: Millburn, New Jersey : Apples & Honey Press, [2023] | Summary:
   "When the animals on Noah's Ark hear a spooky sound, they realize
   there's a goblin in their midst."-- Provided by publisher.
Identifiers: LCCN 2022000411 | ISBN 9781681156026 (hardcover)
Subjects: LCSH: Noah's ark--Juvenile fiction. | Goblins--Juvenile fiction.
   | Animals--Juvenile fiction. | Fear--Juvenile fiction. | CYAC: Noah's
   ark--Fiction. | Goblins--Fiction. | Animals--Fiction. | Fear--Fiction. |
   LCGFT: Animal fiction. | Picture books.
Classification: LCC PZ7.1.T38314 Go 2023 | DDC 813.6 [E]--dc23/eng/20220503
LC record available at https://lccn.loc.gov/2022000411

Designed by Zatar Creative
Edited by Alef Davis
Art directed by Ann D. Koffsky
Printed in China

9 8 7 6 5 4 3 2 1

0524/B2524/A4

It was the animals' first night on Noah's ark.

Noah had brought them aboard two by two.

Outside the rain was pouring down.

Inside the animals were asleep.

All was quiet.

Suddenly the silence was
broken by a strange sound.

WoooOoOoooo

"Was that you, owls?"
the rabbits called.

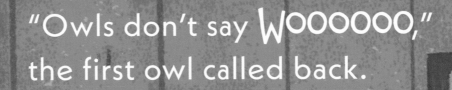

"Owls don't say WOOOOOO," the first owl called back.

"Owls say HOOOOOO," the second owl said.

The strange sound wasn't an owl.

WOOOOOo

The strange sound was getting closer.

"Was that you, cows?" the rabbits called.

"Cows don't say WOOOOOO," the first cow called back.

"Cows say MOOOOOO," the second cow said.

The strange sound wasn't a cow.

WooOoOooooo

Once more that strange sound.
Now it was even closer.

"Was that you, pigeons?" the rabbits called.

"Pigeons don't say WOOOOOO,"
the first pigeon called back.

"Pigeons say COOOOOO,"
the second pigeon said.

The spooky sound
wasn't a pigeon.

Then there was silence.

POooo

"Maybe it's gone," the rabbits said.

AiAiAiAiAiAiAiAii

The rabbits' screams woke the whole ark.

"What's the matter?" the other animals cried. "What's wrong?"

"It's a goblin!" the rabbits screeched. "There's a goblin on the ark!"

"A goblin! Oh, no!"

"We'll light our lights," the fireflies said.
"That will drive the goblin away."

The fireflies lit their lights.

The goblin covered both eyes.

"We'll trumpet our trunks," the elephants said. "That will drive the goblin away."

The elephants trumpeted their trunks.

The goblin covered both ears.

"We'll squirt our scent," the skunks said. "That will certainly drive the goblin away."

The skunks squirted their scent.

The goblin covered both nostrils.

Then came a sound from some other part of the ark.

WooOooOooooo

Instantly the goblin
perked up and
answered *WooOoo*.

"There are two goblins!"
the rabbits exclaimed.

"They're a pair just like us,"
the pigeons said.

"They don't mean us any harm," the owls said.

"They're just trying to find each other," the cows said. "Let's help them."

WooOooOooooo

The second goblin's voice was even fainter now.
The animals could barely hear it.

"Let's make sure the second
goblin can hear *us*,"
the rabbits said.

Then they all gathered around the first goblin.

WooOoo, mooed the cows as loud as they could.

WooOoo, hooted the owls.

WooOoo, cooed the pigeons.

WooOoo, went the fireflies, elephants, and skunks.

WooOoo, answered the second goblin, getting closer now.

More animals began to help.

WooOoo, barked the dogs.

WooOoo, meowed the cats.

WooOoo, croaked the frogs.

WooOoo, roared the lions.

WooOoo, they all went, until—

WooHoo! WooHoo!

The two goblins found each other!

MooooCoooHoooRay!

the animals cheered, and everyone danced around.

Then everyone settled back down to sleep.

Outside, it would rain for forty days and forty nights.

But inside the ark, the animals were safe.

They knew they could count on one another.

Dear Readers,

Everyone knows that Noah's ark had two of each animal on it. But did you know that some traditional interpretations of the story say that there were also goblins on the ark? It makes me wonder: Did the animals on the ark welcome these goblins?

In this story, at first, the animals are too scared of the goblins to welcome them. The goblins look and sound so different from what they're used to. But gradually, the animals realize that the goblins are very much like them. They learn to understand the goblins, and they welcome them to the ark.

Differences can be scary, but they don't have to be. Is there something you used to be scared of, until you learned more about it and understood it better?

Differences can also make our friendships more interesting. Some people are talkative while others are quiet; some are good at sports and others at art. Do you know someone who's different from you, who you'd like to be friends with? What are some things you might do to welcome and include that person?

Shalom,

Susan